Flight of Megizzewas

story by **Karen Trolenberg**

artwork by **Christopher Smith**

From the Author:

The eagle in this book, my Megizzewas (Meh-GIZ-zee-WAHZ), flies over contemporary Michigan scenes, but is named in honor of an eagle rescued in 1917 by my Great-Great-Grandfather, William Adelbert "Deli" Craker.

During the time that Deli loved and cared for his Megizzewas, the bird became one of Omena, Michigan's most famous residents. He drew many visitors, was well known throughout the state, and was featured in many publications. He became a national ambassador for his species when photographs of him were used by the National Audubon Society in literature calling for the protection of the bald eagle. Deli's Megizzewas flew to his freedom in 1931.

It is my hope that my Megizzewas will continue the legacy of his namesake by also acting as an ambassador for his species. May he spark a love and appreciation of bald eagles and their habitats in the hearts and minds of all who read this story, and for many generations to come.

Megizzewas means "young eagle" in Anishinaabemowin, a language spoken by native people of the Michigan area. Various spellings and pronunciations are acceptable. I chose the spelling used by my Great-Great-Grandfather.

Karen Trolenberg

Flight of Megizzewas by Karen Trolenberg
Illustrations by Christopher Smith
Design by Jenifer Thomas
Printing by Quad Graphics

All inquires should be addressed to:
Grand Bird Books
P.O. Box 215, Northport MI 49670
E-mail: grandbirdbooks@gmail.com

Special Thanks to:
Brad Trolenberg
Allen Kalchik
Sharon Kalchik
Janet Novak
Tim Kaufman

For ordering information or to contact Karen Trolenberg visit
www.karentrolenberg.com

To view more artwork by Christopher Smith visit
www.chrissmithart.com

To contact Jenifer Thomas visit
www.drawbigdesign.com

First Edition

Published by Grand Bird Books
Northport, Michigan

Printed ISBN-13: 978-0-692-25248-2

Library of Congress Control Number: 2015900836

Flight of Megizzewas

story by Karen Trolenberg

artwork by Christopher Smith

Megizzewas flies high over the land called Michigan.

He flies above an apple orchard where a boy is picking apples.

The boy waves and calls out, "Hello, Megizzewas!"
Megizzewas tips his wings and screeches in reply.

He flies above a meadow where a family of deer has gathered.

The doe grazes on green grasses while her fawns frolic nearby. The buck lifts his head and snorts when he sees the shadow of Megizzewas gliding across the meadow.

He flies above a lake where a canoe skims across the surface.

Megizzewas flaps his powerful wings and soars through the air with ease. The people in the canoe paddle hard to get to their destination on the distant shore.

He flies above a river where people are fishing for trout.

Megizzewas swoops down to catch a fish of his own.
This one will make a fine supper.

He flies above the sand dunes where
children are climbing all the way to the top.

Megizzewas circles around to see them laughing as they tumble back down.

He flies above the Straits of Mackinac.

Megizzewas stops to rest atop the
south tower of the Mackinac Bridge.
Ships travel under the bridge and
cars travel over the bridge
all day and all night.

The Mighty Mac never
needs to sleep, but
Megizzewas does.

So, as the sun slips closer to the western horizon,
he starts the long flight back to his nest.

Sleep well, children…
with sandy hair and sun-tanned noses.

Sleep well, fishermen…
with full bellies, and stories to tell.

Sleep well, paddlers…
with strong arms and many more journeys to take.

Sleep well, deer…
with heads curled 'round legs on cozy grass beds.

Sleep well, young man…
with big dreams and a lifetime of discoveries to make.

Now rest your tired wings to fly again
tomorrow, and sleep well, Megizzewas...

Sleep well.